# The Dragon of Og
## Rumer Godden

*illustrated by Pauline Baynes*

M

*This book is for Anthony*
*who now owns the Dragon's Pool*

ISBN 0 333 31731 9

*First published 1981 by*
MACMILLAN CHILDREN'S BOOKS
A division of Macmillan Publishers Limited
*London and Basingstoke*

*Associated companies throughout the world*

*Composition by Filmtype Services Limited, Scarborough, England*

Printed in Italy by New Interlitho S.p.A. - Milan

**British Library Cataloguing in Publication Data**

Godden, Rumer
    The dragon of Og.
    I. Title     II. Baynes, Pauline
    823'. 914[J]     PZ7.G54

    ISBN 0-333-31731-9

The Angus Og of this story was not the Angus Og, Lord of the Isles, though he would have liked to be. Nor was he one of the famous prize bulls, all called Angus Og who win the Highland Championship. He might have been the ancestor of the lovable ruffian Angus Og of the Scottish *Daily Record* strip cartoon but he was a chieftain with a small estate or demesne just over the Border between England and Scotland on the Scottish side.

I t happened long ago in the lowlands of Scotland in the days when castles were made of wood; this particular Castle of Tundergarth stood on a hill above fields and meadows that were ringed with forest; most forests around castles were cut with wide tracks called 'swathes' so that the chieftains could see when enemies were coming; the enemies were usually other lord chieftains and their men or else, in winter, wolves – wild boar and lynxes lived in the forests too – but the Lords of Tundergarth did not bother about swathes. For one thing, between their meadows and the forest there ran a wide river called the Water of Milk but it was not as mild as it sounds because in the biggest of its pools, below a deep dark cave, lived a dragon.

He had come there long before there was any castle, only a cluster of turf and wattle huts on the top of the hill. His mother had brought him one moonlight night while everyone was asleep.

When the time is ripe for a she-dragon to have children she gives a strange wandering cry; the he-dragons hear it and at once fly up in the sky to fight one another to see who will be the one to answer her. Most he-dragons spend their time fighting one another to the death which is why there are so few; the she-ones stay on earth but when the winner comes down to mate, his passion is so fierce that he often kills her with love. This Dragon's Mother, though, was strong and she was soon able to go and find a sandy place near a loch which is Scottish for a lake – the place had to be near water – and scoop out a hollow where she laid her eggs. He-dragons take no interest in eggs, nor in their sons or daughters and the Dragon never knew his Father.

It takes a thousand days for a dragon-egg to hatch, ten thousand more for the worm that crawls out of the egg to become even a baby dragon – dragons count in hundreds and thousands – two thousand weeks more until he was, as it were, in his teens, so that his Mother, who had watched over this one for so long had grown deeply fond of him – he was the only one of her eggs that had hatched – and she was most particular, when he was a full he-dragon, as to where she put him. She had to put him somewhere because she knew there was another little dragon, or dragons, on the way and, "One is enough," she said. Dragons like to stay in one place all their lives so she had to choose carefully and for weeks she roamed the land until at last she found the pool and the cave above it; both were deep and quiet and the people, the cottars, who lived in the huts, seemed to be going about their business, too occupied to harry a dragon – dragons spend their lives being harried. "It's all those stories and legends," the Mother Dragon told her son. "You should be all right here but, above all, don't offend the people. Don't try and take after your Uncle."

The Uncle was a dashing dragon and beautiful with colours of emerald green, turquoise and royal blue in his scales; he had golden claws, a great golden crest and wings lined with ruby-red. The young Dragon's crest was only just growing, his wings were still small and his colours still pale but his Uncle encouraged him, and said, "Soon you will be able to throw flames from your nostrils."

"Will I?" asked the young Dragon, astonished and dazzled.

"Of course," said Uncle, "and they grow hotter with practice. You must practise and now that you are almost full grown, refuse to eat anything else but young girls."

"Do dragons eat girls?" asked the Dragon, still more astonished.

"Of course, all through history," said Uncle. "Always have, always will," and now, "Would it offend the villagers?" the Dragon asked his Mother, "if I ate their daughters?" He was still young, only five hundred years old, and did not know the ways of the world. "If I ate just one, now and then?"

"I believe it would," said his Mother, "so don't," and the

Dragon didn't but, after he came to Tundergarth, he said, "I wish they wouldn't come and do their washing in the river, especially when they turn their petticoats up. Their legs are so pink and white." There was no one to listen except the squirrels because nobody dared come too near: the girls now did their washing far upstream; even the cottar children, who are incurably curious, kept away from the river bank when they were watching the cattle – there were no fences then so the cattle had to be herded. Sometimes the bolder children crept up and hid behind the rocks but it was seldom they saw anything, and then it was just a crest, or a claw, the end of a tail or a shadow, and as the villagers found he bothered no one, they grew proud of their dragon. "He keeps enemies away. He makes the crops grow. He is our luck," and certainly the Lords of Tundergarth grew rich and soon, up on the hill, they cleared away the huts and built their Castle.

The Dragon saw its wooden walls rising where the turf huts had been. The huts were down below now, in what was called the 'bailey', a wide enclosure behind a high stockade. Outside the bailey were other wooden houses, each with its farm and fields where the chief men-at-arms and the craftsmen lived. The chief house was the Seneschal's, second only to the Castle; the Seneschal looked after the Castle, the land and the people when the Lord was away fighting; he also watched over the Dragon.

He-dragons usually live in caves, she-dragons in water, but because he loved his mother better than his uncle, however

dashing, the Dragon chose to live in the pool of the Water of Milk, "And no one is to disturb him," ordered the Seneschal. All the same, the boys and girls sometimes dared one another to throw stones into the pool hoping they would rouse him.

Even if the children had roused him they were perfectly safe; a cottar child could not have tempted the hungriest dragon. They usually ran about almost naked, not only in summer but in the bitter winter cold, so that their skins were like leather, thick and grimy; their hair was matted – it was never brushed – their eyes always red because, in the huts where they lived, the one room had no chimney so it was full of smoke from the hearth and cooking fires. Their noses were always running from the cold and they often had sores. "Ugh!" said the Dragon, but not unkindly – it never entered his head that the stones were meant for him; he had not understood, then, that humans could be unkind, but from long years of being alone he had grown shy. True, every two or three weeks he would come up and fly over the meadows to pounce on a bullock, but only once every two or three weeks – he was not a greedy Dragon and it was always when the children were not looking – they often tired of watching the cattle so the girls picked wild flowers or quarrelled or gossipped while the boys made bows and arrows, or slings to throw pebbles, or fished with their home-made lines and hooks. Then the Dragon would open his wings noiselessly and quick as a wink fly over the meadow to his chosen bullock. He had learned that he had only to make a beast look up into his green dragon eyes and it would walk towards him as if in a dream, straight into his claws. These eyes are part of dragon-power; his Mother had taught him that. "But don't stare at anyone unless you want to harm them," she told him.

"Who should I want to harm?" asked the Dragon. The bullock did not even know it had been harmed. When it had been snatched up in his claws and taken into the river, one scrunch and it was gone.

Dragons eat all they want at one meal, then they go to sleep. "I'll let my dinner rest," the Dragon would say and sink down to the bottom of his pool. After two or even three weeks he would wake up feeling fine and frisky. This is the time when, if a dragon is bad, he can be dangerous, but Tundergarth's Dragon only wanted to play. Unfortunately there was no one to play with.

His mother had decided it was better not to visit him. "It would only unsettle you and might upset the people."

"Uncle?" asked the Dragon wistfully.

"Uncle would upset them worse. No, you're old enough now to manage on your own."

"All alone?" the Dragon was more wistful still but, "All alone," said his mother firmly.

Poor Dragon! He was not on play-terms with the cottar children and if any other humans caught a glimpse of him, they screamed and ran away so he learned that it was better, when he came up from his pool, to lie on the forest side of the bank, but he often looked wistfully at the meadow bank and its flowers, "I have never smelled a flower," thought the Dragon.

He tried to talk to the squirrels but they chattered too much to listen. Sometimes they threw him nuts but as soon as he turned his head away they scampered down to take them back again. The only visitors who came near were flies in summer – bothersome like the cottar children but, like them, to be expected. Butterflies came too, attracted by his colours but they were too busy with their flit and flutter to stay for more than a few seconds; as for the fish in the pool, they had no conversation at all and soon – that is to say in two or three hundred years – the Dragon grew so shy that if he did hear anyone coming – dragon ears are so sharp they can even hear the smallest barefoot child – he would plunge into his pool and hide.

The Dragon came to full dragonhood when he was nine hundred years old; his crest was high – it ran from his head, all along his back to the end of his tremendous tail; his wings had grown but he never thought of using them to fly into the sky and fight other dragons; as far as he knew he was the only dragon in the world and he lived peaceably in the pool of the Water of Milk. In spring, summer, autumn, he came up on the bank to lie in the sun or rain, usually in the rain – at Tundergarth it rained far more than the sun shone – but the Dragon liked the rain; it was warmer than the pool water and trickled under his scales so that it was like having a refreshing shower. In winter he did what the squirrels did, curled up and hushed, which was just as well as the cattle seldom came down to the meadows; they stayed in their byre beside the hut's one room, and their midden helped to keep it warm. On the rare sunny days, the Dragon might wake and crack the ice to make a breathing hole for the fish with his tail – a dragon's tail is so powerful it can crack the thickest ice – and if the cattle were let out he might take a bullock, though in winter they grew pitifully thin.

If he stayed above water his scales and wings were sometimes rimed – outlined with frost; then he shone and looked gorgeous though he did not know it, and, "Grrh! I'm getting chilblains all along my crest," said the Dragon and sank quickly under the water again; often in those winters, "I wish, I wish I had learned how to flame," he said, "then I could light me my own little bonfire," but, try as he would, he was not able to flame; his Uncle had not told him he had to get angry first.

It was on his nine-hundredth birthday, though of course the Dragon did not know it was his birthday, that the last of the Lords of Tundergarth died, the end of a long long line of Tundergarth fathers and sons and the Castle and its lands went to his nephew in the far North, Angus Og.

Not easily; Angus Og had to fight other chieftains for his

rights, but he was used to fighting; he had trouble with the people of Tundergarth too. Donald McDonald was Seneschal then and, "I'll not give me allegiance to any Og – and him a Highlander," said Donald. In the end he had to, as had all the people – Angus Og was not a man to be gainsayed, except sometimes by his young wife Matilda and the Castle became the Castle and demesne of Og. "The Castle of Og! Hech ay man!" sighed Donald. "Og! I ask ye!" but the Dragon did not mind. He had heard the cottar children talking of great changes but 'Dragon of Tundergarth', 'Dragon of Og' – it made no difference to him. At least, that is what he thought.

On a wet windy day of March, in spring-time – "new time", the people and the Dragon should have said – at last Angus Og came marching through the forest to take possession of his Castle.

Angus Og was a big man – though perhaps not quite as big as he believed – with a head of red hair and a thick red beard and a voice that was used to roaring. With him came his men and his new young wife, Matilda. Angus Og had a great war horse – bigger than a shire or cart horse while the Lady Matilda rode a jennett – a pretty little horse dappled grey she had brought from England.

No one could see Matilda; she was huddled in a great frieze cloak and hood; only her small hands in gauntlets showed holding the reins, but she guided her jennett firmly.

The men-at-arms had riding horses; the rest cantered on ponies and there was a long train of pack-horses carrying goods, mostly Matilda's. When Donald warned Angus Og not to cross the river, "Pish!" said Angus Og which, in Scotland, is worse than rude.

The Dragon wondered why the Water of Milk had suddenly turned murky, more like ale than milk; it was from the mud churned up by the horses – and why had it grown smelly – that was from the dung the horses dropped. He heard the cavalcade coming long before he saw it: the crashing as the men hewed down the trees with their axes: the high note of a bagpipe: the horns calling the hounds in, the hounds themselves baying: the cries, not war cries but cries of triumph as the men of Og marched down. The Dragon was too shy to come up on the bank but he brought his eyes level with the water and saw the great cavalcade; everyone was too taken up with it to notice his crest.

Angus Og had never had a castle before, "And it's lucky ye are to have one now," said Donald. "If my Lord had had a son. . . ."

"I shall have a son," said Angus Og and he boasted, " and I shall make this Castle the best in the land, better than King David's."

"We'll see," said Donald, which in Scots language means that it will never happen, but it did happen, "And in a flicker," said Donald, which is how it seemed to him. "Hech ay, man!" sighed Donald, but was it Angus Og's doing or was it the Lady Matilda's?

"She? She's but a slip of a lass," said Donald's wife, Edith.

"Ay, she's that, but. . . ." and Donald grew more and more gloomy.

At first Matilda found the Castle gloomy too and unbearably bleak. It was dirty, with dank rushes on the floor and a haze of wood smoke from the great hearth: its chimney-flue was cracked and never cleaned. "It's all so dark and so uncomfortable," said Matilda. The people were rough and uncouth and she could not understand their talk. Angus Og was often away fighting or hunting and she was as lonely as the Dragon. When the rain beat against the walls and the wind seemed to wail around the castle, and everywhere outside seemed mud or dung, Matilda could have sat down and cried, but she was not one for sitting or crying and soon, "I do see," said Edith, and, "Ay", said Donald, and sighed, "Such stramash and bother!"

"It'll be bonny when it's done," said Edith but Donald was not to be won over and, "Ye're as much comfort as a cat on a hot griddle," was all he said.

The first thing Lady Matilda did was to clean the inner court in the Castle of its midden – the huge spread of manure the horses and cattle made when they were driven in for shelter from the snow – or from wars. "But the midden keeps the Castle warm," objected Angus Og.

"It stinks," Matilda wrinkled up her little nose; when she did that, to Angus Og she was so pretty he could not argue any further. "Besides, I want to plant roses," said Matilda. "The rose of Scotland would grow here," said Matilda, "the little white rose that smells sharp and sweet and maybe the red and white striped Latin rose and briar roses; and, talking of middens," said Matilda, "would you please ask your people not to squat down by the walls. We shall have privies," – which are lavatories – and she promised, "My hangings will keep you warm," and soon tales came down from the Castle of what the villagers had not seen or thought of before, of hangings on the Castle walls, tapestries woven or embroidered with story pictures in colours of blue and rose and red and green. Anyone who saw them could not stop looking at them but, "Such nonsense," said the women. "She and her haivers." They called Matilda 'she'.

"*She* has clean rushes put down on the floor every week."

"Every *week*! It used to be once a year."

"*She* makes us wash the platters every time they're used."

"What's wrong with wiping them with a nip of bread?"

"And all the vessels too. *She* says they're greasy."

The vessels now were not just wood or earthenware, some were of brass or even silver. "Might be gold," whispered the women. "*She* makes us polish them."

"Ay, and the furniture too, tables and chairs, stools and settles, with the best beeswax."

*She* had embroidered a red cushion for Angus Og's great chair but *she* would not let him tear his meat with his hands; he had to cut it with his horn-handled knife as did all who sat at table in the great hall, "And you will please not throw your bones over your shoulder on to the floor for the dogs," said Matilda.

"How will the poor things eat?" roared Angus Og.

"The dogs will be fed in the kennels," and, "Did you ever hear the likes of that?" asked the women. "*She* and her pernickety ways," but the Castle began to have a different smell, fresh and clean. Matilda had had the chimney mended with wattle and plaster so there was less smoke; fragrance came too from bunches of herbs Matilda strung from the ceiling and, slowly, the women began to have a pride in her. Of their own accord they washed their feet before they came in – they all of them went barefoot – and, "She will not let her Lord walk into the great hall in his miry boots," they said, wishing they could make their men do likewise. For the first time in his life Angus Og felt what it was like to wear slippers.

"Isn't it comfortable?" asked Matilda.

It was wonderfully comfortable. "But it doesn't become me," growled Angus Og.

"It does," said Matilda and, indeed, when, after the tables had been cleared, she fetched her harp and, sitting on a stool, with it on her knees, played and sang to Angus Og as he sat in his great chair by the fire, he looked a different man with a smile in his eyes and a soft look on his face as he listened and pulled the ears of his favourite wolf-hound Brag, but gently, gently.

Not content with plenishing up the inside of the Castle, Matilda changed the outside too. She had the top of the hill levelled and planted an orchard with cherries, pears and plums and between the trees had paths made, smooth for walking.

"*She* likes to walk," said the women who never sat down for ten minutes unless they were at their looms or spinning. "Walking, and what is she doing? Nothing."

"Everything," Matilda could have said. Most people think when someone walks slowly, not talking, but feeling the wind, watching birds and flowers – at night, stars – he or she is being plain idle, whereas what they are doing is most important of all: thinking. As she walked along, Matilda was planning and shaping ideas in her mind; sometimes she said a prayer, sometimes she sang quietly, but she was not idle. She even liked to walk in the rain – like the Dragon she found it exhilarating. She wore her cloak and hood and she soon saw why the women went barefoot – her pattens, wooden and high, sank in the mud and it was easier to wash feet than pattens. "A lady bare-footed!" The women were shocked but the rainy days were the best of all because then Matilda could count on being quite alone – especially beside the river. The cottar children huddled under the trees or made themselves shelters of straw though in any case they would not have pestered Matilda; had she not ordered, "Every child herding the cattle is to come up to the Castle before it goes out in the morning and get a bannock of barley bread and a good sup of milk." The children would have died for Lady Matilda but they were in such awe of her – she was so beautiful and clean – that they kept away.

Angus Og had made the walk along the river for Matilda.

"I wonder ye're not afeart for her to walk so close to the river," Donald told Angus Og.

"Och! Nothing will hurt Matilda," said Angus Og. "She can charm the very birds off the trees. She can even tame a wolf."

"It's not birds or wolves I'm thinking of," said Donald. "It's the Dragon. It's said they're very partial to young women," but Angus Og still said, "Pish!"

It was more than a year after she had come to the Castle that, on a May day, one of Og's rare sunny days, Matilda, walking beside the river in the sweet warm air, stopped and caught her breath; there, on the opposite bank, was the Dragon fast asleep. He had grown into a beautiful dragon, far more beautiful than his Uncle; his scales were more emerald, more turquoise and royal blue, his crest and his claws more golden, the lining of his wings, if he had unfolded them, a deeper ruby red, his tail so long that it stretched from the bank to the river.

Matilda stepped so lightly that her shoes – that afternoon she was wearing them – did not bend as much as a blade of grass and the Dragon had not heard her; his golden eyelashes were still shut over his eyes. "Then there really and truly is a Dragon," breathed Matilda. The river had a line of stepping stones and she lifted up the long hem of her gown and began to step across, but she disturbed a pebble and it splashed into the stream. The Dragon opened one eye and then he opened the other. They grew wider and wider because he had never seen a human like this, a human as beautiful as himself.

Matilda's white head kerchief that fell over her shoulders showed her hair which was golden as his crest. Her white dress had gold crossings and parted to show a ruby red kirtle. Her eyes were as green as his own and, though he could not help staring, they did not draw her in as they did with the bullocks; she only looked back at him unafraid, indeed as if her eyes were smiling. What was more, she spoke to him in dragon language that has no sound. "Hullo," said Lady Matilda.

It was too much for the Dragon; he plunged off the bank into his pool making such a splash that he sent up a spray of drops soaking Matilda. This was not gallant but Matilda understood. Poor fellow, she thought, perhaps no one has spoken to him for a long long time – she did not know that no one had ever spoken to him. When she had dried herself in the sun, she went back to the

other bank and picked a nosegay of wild flowers, marguerites and poppies – they grew then in the meadows – trefoil and clover that smelled of honey. She bound them together with a braid from her hair, crossed the stepping stones again and put the flowers where the Dragon had slept.

When she had gone and the cottar children were far off in the distance the Dragon came out of his pool and found the nosegay. "For me?" he asked. He could not believe it but, as he looked round he knew it could be for no one else because there was no one else. "Somebody has made me a nosegay," said the Dragon. "Then somebody likes me." The squirrels who had been watching it all chattered their teeth as if they were telling him nobody could but, "She likes me!" said the Dragon and he smiled. Then, to his own surprise, two tears slid down his scaly cheeks, one from each eye; the tears were like pearls as big as ripe pears; they went plop on the pebbles. "She likes me."

Meanwhile Angus Og had conquered two other demesnes but far from being satisfied with his new lands, Angus Og grew more rumbustious and greedy and more and more proud. He told Donald he wanted a counting up of his people, men, women and children. "They'll nae like that," said Donald. "It's treating them like cattle. It'll be the cattle next," said Donald.

It was the cattle, "And they must be counted every month," ordered Angus Og.

"There's two missing," roared Angus Og.

They had rounded up the bullocks and counted them. "Two missing."

"There is not," said Donald. "Ye've reckoned without our Dragon."

"Our *Dragon?*" Angus Og was so dumbfounded that he spoke almost quietly.

"Ay," said Donald, unperturbed. "He usually takes two; this month he only took one. Seems off his food."

"The Dragon?"

"Ay."

"Stop saying 'Ay' and explain."

"I tell't you. Twice every month, or maybe once the Dragon takes a bullock," said Donald. "Always has, always will."

"He will not!" bellowed Angus Og. "They're mine," and, "A bullock every three weeks," he exploded to Lady Matilda.

"I don't call that much," said Matilda. "You take one every day, or the flesher does for you and your men, and the Dragon buries his all out of sight; *he* doesn't throw bones about," but Angus Og told Donald that the bullocks and sheep were not to graze by the river any more. "I'll keep what is mine," said Angus Og. "That's how to build a realm. I shall be a greater noble than King David."

"Ye'll not do that by being parsimonious," said Donald.

"Parsimonious? What is that?"

"Downright mean," said Donald. "If the Dragon gets

hungry he might come marauding. Why, man!" – Donald was too
upset to address his Lord as a Seneschal should – "Why, man! If a
dragon is angry he can breathe out flames and fireballs. He could
set the whole place alight, bailey and farms and the Castle."

"Pish!" said Angus Og.

"He might take a child."

"Well, we have too many children," said Angus Og.
"Even you could not count them."

He was not as hard-hearted as he sounds; Angus Og was
fond of children; he patted them on their heads and let them look
in his pockets for the honey-fudge Matilda made and that he
carried there for them. He would even lift them up and let them
ride on his saddle-bow – not the cottar children, they were too
dirty and smelly – but his chiefmen's boys and girls. "One day I
must give him a little Angus Og of his own, or a little Matilda,"
said Matilda. As a matter of fact, Angus Og did not know quite
what to believe or to do about the Dragon and the bullock and so,
"Don't let it happen again," he told Donald, but of course it
happened again.

"I saw it," bellowed Angus Og. "Saw it with my own
eyes."

Matilda sighed. It was she who had taught the Dragon to
come out in the open and not be so shy.

For some days after the nosegay, the Dragon had not been
hungry at all, he had taken the flowers down into the pool and lay
looking at them and smelling them as content as if he were full of
bullock – more content – and when, at last, he had come up to the
bank he had felt fresh and frisky as never before.

Matilda had been down to the river and called several times without as much as a ripple in answer but now, when she came, he greeted her with a breath of delight; a dragon's breath is a fuff of such power that even across the river it blew her skirts over her head, but she only laughed. Then, leaving her shoes on the meadow, quite unafraid she had come to him over the stepping stones. The Dragon had not plunged away because, as she stepped, Matilda talked to him, the first time any human had and, "Thank you for the wee bunch," the Dragon managed at last to say about the flowers.

"It was a pleasure," said Matilda and she stayed with him on the pebbles, talking. "But you mustn't blow my skirts over my head again," she told the Dragon. "My Lord would not like it," but as the Dragon had not met 'my Lord' – otherwise Angus Og – this meant little to him and, as he talked and played with Matilda, he could not resist, every now and then, giving a little fuff. "It's your legs. They're such dainties," he said.

"I wonder you don't eat me," Matilda teased him, but the Dragon did not understand teasing.

"Eat you! My Lady!" and he laid his great scaly head with its gold crest at her bare feet and, again, two tears rolled from his eyes on to the pebbles and, again, they were like two pearls.

Matilda forebore to tease him any more and soon she was able to entice him to the other bank where, if it was fine weather, they played and gambolled – few people have gambolled with a dragon; he kept his claws in and was careful with his tail. When they were tired they sat down on the grass and Matilda sang to him. She made him a crown too out of a daisy-chain.

It was too peaceful to last and, "I saw it," said Angus Og. "The Dragon. Saw it with my own eyes."

"'Him', not 'it'," said Matilda.

Angus Og had been carousing with his neighbouring Lord – though Og's nearest neighbour, the Lord of Castle Corrie, was ten miles away. He was one of the few chieftains with whom Angus Og did not fight; they were friends and he had stayed so late that his men had gone home taking the dogs, except Brag, and the torches with them. The torches did not matter – it was full moonlight – but Angus was glad of Brag because the forest at night is mysterious and when he came out above the river Brag had started his great bay. "It was no-canny av'a," – which means uncanny – Angus Og told Matilda. "Right eerie, and then I saw it . . ."

"Him," said Matilda, but Angus Og went on. "At first I thought I had taken too much wine, but no; I saw it spread its wings and this great shape came down, its eyes like green lamps. Those fousome brats of children had left some bullocks out – I'll skin them – and one bullock went towards it, walked of its own will, if you please, up to those eyes as if the bullock was dreaming. Then I saw claws snatch it up, then back to the river and one scrunch and the bullock was gone. One of our finest Galloways," swore Angus Og.

Indeed it was one of the best and tasted delicious; after it the Dragon sank into his pool. "I'll let my dinner rest," but Angus Og would not let him rest.

"That Dragon must be killed," said Angus Og.

"Killed? Our Dragon?" Donald was stunned.

"Yes," bellowed Angus Og.

"Ye cannae kill our Dragon. He's Tundergarth's – I mean Og's – luck."

"Pish!"

"Ye'll be in for trouble," said Donald. "Even if it's just a sticky cake."

"A sticky cake! The very thing!" and Angus Og rubbed his hands in glee.

"What's a sticky cake?" asked Matilda.

"An old old way of catching dragons," explained Edith. "Ye make it of honey and breadcrumbs to entice him like – and in it ye melt some rozet" – which is resin – "so it gets right claggy" – which means gluey.

"And then you put some pitch," said Angus Og. "He'll not taste that because of the sweetness, but if he flames the pitch'll catch fire inside him and he'll explode."

"No! No!" cried Matilda, but, "I have never known our Dragon flame," Edith whispered to her. "He'll not explode."

"Even if he doesnae flame, it'll stick his jaws tight shut so he cannae eat," objected Donald.

"At least he'll die natural," said Edith.

"Ha! Ha!" said Angus Og. "We'll make the sticky cake and put it on the bank."

"But that's cruel," blazed Matilda. "Far more cruel than killing him outright," but Angus Og only said, "Ha!"

"They have made you a sticky cake," Matilda told the Dragon. "My Lord and the Seneschal Donald and all the Castle cooks. A sticky cake."

The Dragon was enormously flattered. "But how kind! How very kind."

"It isn't kind at all," said Matilda and explained about the sticky cake. "You mustn't touch a crumb of it," but the Dragon was so flattered he did not want to listen.

"Couldn't I give it just a lick?"

"No! No!" cried Matilda, but the Dragon gave the cake a good lick. It was as big as a cart-wheel and smelled of honey and prunes and raisins and other good things as it lay on the bank but, being as obedient to Matilda as he had been to his Mother, the Dragon did not eat a crumb – but he licked and licked; he did not catch fire as he still had not learnt to flame but in half an hour his tongue was stuck to the roof of his mouth. The squirrels laughed and the Dragon dived into his pool in terror.

I must move that cake, thought Matilda, and she called the cottar children; they came in their dozens, stood the big cake on end and wheeled it into the meadow. Matilda had called them to move it but she did not dream they would eat it – they were so hungry they did not even taste the pitch. The cake was so big, the sweetness so good that they shouted to the other children, even Donald's grandchildren, who came running. They all ate the cake down to the last crumb, the crumb Matilda had forbidden to the Dragon, while she wrung her hands and watched. It was no use saying 'Don't,' and, "I suppose their mothers can unstick them," said Matilda.

A strange quietness settled on Og – there were no shrill voices, no shrieks or screams or crying, no laughter. "Oh, wow! What is the matter?" cried the mothers. "Tell me or I'll shake ye," but it was no use shaking. The children's jaws were stuck tight.

"Speak! Speak!" and the children tried. "Tuth-th-uth-luth-h-uth."

"Oh wow! My dearie, my poor wee thing, what happened?" wept each mother. "Try and tell what happened." The children tried desperately but all that came out was, "Luth-th-luth-huth-uth." The cottar children grunted through their runny noses like piglets. "My dearie! My poor wee thing," wailed the mothers.

"You and your sticky cake!" Angus Og stormed at Donald.

"Mine? It was yer's."

"It was your idea. You put it there."

"Ye perfidious slidderie feartie ..." began Donald, but Angus Og was not listening.

"I think I'll have a few days' hunting," he told Matilda. "There's too many boar in the forest. I need to sort them."

Matilda did not speak but her look, like Donald's, said, "Coward."

The cleverer mothers found a way to make a little hole in the sticky so that their children could suck milk or thin broth through a bit of straw or a reed, and as their mouths were shut so tightly, their own warmth gradually melted the resin and pitch – which was not to say they did not have tummy aches. "Serves ye right," said the mothers who, as they grew less frightened, were cross. "That'll learn ye not to be greedy."

The cottar mothers copied the little holes and Matilda provided the milk and broth but it still took time – the cottar children were not as warm as the other children. Then, at Matilda's suggestion, the mothers picked short willow twigs and frayed the ends so that they made a little brush to brush away the last traces of the sticky. These were the first toothbrushes in Scotland, maybe Britain; before then no mother had said what they almost always say now when it is bedtime, "Mind you brush your teeth."

Matilda was worried about the children, but more worried about the Dragon who had no mother to help him; indeed he had retreated into his pool where the coolness of the water made the sticky harder. It was days before Matilda could coax him out into the sun where it might melt. "It's only your tongue," she said, but it was not only his tongue; the Dragon was upset in his feelings. "I thought they were being kind," he said, "but they were only pretending." He could speak because his words did not need to sound. "Pretending with me, their Dragon!" He was angry and, suddenly, to his and Matilda's amazement, a flame came out of his nostril, not a big one, not long or bright or hot, but a flame.

The Dragon was so amazed he sat down on his haunches to look. "I didn't know I could do that, though Uncle said I would," and another came from his other nostril. Then both.

"Be careful! Be careful!" cried Matilda. "There might be some pitch or resin left in you. You might explode."

"I'll show them explode!" said the Dragon. "Mean unkind traitors," and he breathed two longer, brighter, hotter flames.

"Splendid!" Matilda could not help saying it, nor help clapping her hands but, "Keep out of the way, my Lady," said the Dragon in a way Matilda had not known before. "I might scorch you. Unkind! Traitors!" and he sent out such flames that the squirrels had to leap for safety out of their trees.

"Splendid," said Matilda again, "but now die down," and she laid her hand on the Dragon's head which immediately calmed him. "All the same," said Matilda, "I'm glad you have learnt to flame."

"I'll practise," promised the Dragon, but it is tiring being angry, especially on an empty stomach and soon the Dragon went to sleep.

For a long time the cottar children were too weak from the sticky cake to herd cattle so the men had to do it and, after some days of pondering about the Dragon – it was only the thought of Matilda that made Angus Og ponder at all – he ordered the men, "You will drive the cattle away from the meadows up to the top fields, far off from the river, every last beast of them."

"There'll be mischief," warned Donald. "Worse trouble."

The Dragon had had to go without food for a long time because of his stuck tongue and when, at last, he came up to eat, he was hungry as never before. "Starving!" said the Dragon, but what did he see in the meadows? Nothing but meadow. There was not a bullock or cow or calf, not the least little lamb, not even a rabbit – the rabbits had sensed something would happen and gone into their burrows. The Dragon looked and looked but in the afternoon light everything was empty. It was too early for the cattle to be driven home and, "They have taken away my dinner! All my dinners!" he cried and from his nostrils shot flames that reached far across the meadows and scorched a burnt track in the grass.

The Dragon did not go marauding as Donald had feared, as his Uncle and Mother certainly would have done, seizing a tender fat child, or a toothsome maiden; that did not occur to him and he turned back to his pool, but he was so angry and hurt that he flamed hotter and hotter and soon the water in the pool was boiling. Nor did the flames die down: every time he thought of bullock the flames grew hotter still. To try and cool himself he swam all night from pool to pool up and down the river, and in each one the water began to seethe and bubble.

Early next morning hubbub broke out all along the river. Matilda heard it and woke Angus Og who seized his cloak and wrapped it round him – he slept naked. He leapt out of bed. "What in the devil's name now?" and, rushing out of doors he met Donald running up the orchard path and wailing, "The salmon! The salmon."

"The salmon?" Angus Og stopped.

"Ay. The salmon and all the trout."

"What about the salmon and the trout? Speak man."

"Cooked. Cooked." Donald was near to sobbing. "Cooked and floating on the water."

"Who cooked them?"

"The Dragon ... his breath. It set the water boiling. Och! You should have spared him his bullock." Donald turned to Angus Og. "We, with the finest fishing in all the Lowlands. All cooked. The folk are eating them now."

"They are meant for eating." Matilda in her frieze cloak over her night-robe had followed Angus Og.

"Not for the likes of them." Donald was truly sobbing now. "The finest fishing and not one left. Not one."

"But this is heronious, outrageous." Angus Og had turned almost pale. "All?" He could hardly speak. "All gone?"

"Ay. The people are gobbling them up. Every man jack of them, and the women and children too."

Indeed they were. It was raining, the drizzle that Scots people call a smurr, but the people took no notice. The good river water had cooked the fish, "To a turn," as Matilda said. The Castle steward managed to save a few for Matilda and Angus Og, but men, women and children were eating their fill; even the cottars, who had usually to be content with minnows or a bit of tough pike were eating the lovely pink salmon flesh and learning the delicate taste of a trout. Soon somebody brought down a barrel of ale, another of mead – it could be guessed that was at the orders of Lady Matilda. "As this has happened, let's enjoy it," she said of the fish, and such a feast had never been known in Tundergarth, and, "God bless Og!" shouted the people and, "Bless our Dragon!" The Dragon had eaten a few of the salmon himself, though it was rather like eating his friends and, as his anger and his hunger were appeased, he had gone back to sleep, but, "I'll have it's blood for this," swore Angus Og.

"It shall be slain," said Angus Og.

"Never," said Matilda and clung to him. "My Lord, if you love me . . ." but Angus Og put her out of the way.

"My Lord."

"Hush woman!" Angus Og had never called her 'woman' before but Matilda knelt and caught his hand.

"Angus!"

"Wheesht-up," said Angus Og roughly – he had never been rough with Matilda but now he roared, "Do you want me to lock you in your room?"

"I would climb out of the window."

"Not if I set Edith over you," and, "Am I not your Lord?" roared Angus Og. "I said it should be slain and slain it will be." He had come to like that word better than 'killed'; it sounded more fierce. "I'll slay it myself."

"Nae lad, I mean, my Lord," said Donald. "That would never do."

"Why wouldn't it do?" Angus Og was offended.

"Ye wouldn't last two minutes, that's why," said Donald.

"A Dragon is a royal beast," Matilda said through her tears, "and has to be killed – slain – royally."

"And am not I royal?"

"No, ye're not," said Donald.

"There is only one person," said Matilda, "who knows how to kill a dragon and that is a Knight."

"One of those Norman popinjays?"

"Yes – and they're not popinjays."

"Am'nt I as good as a Knight?"

"You haven't been trained," said Matilda. "A Knight knows just where to strike and, for another thing, you haven't the weapons."

"I have my good axe and my spear."

"Ye need a sword," said Donald, and Matilda went on, "And you haven't the armour."

"My helmet and jacket, that's good chain mail and my shield."

"Made of leather. How could that help ye against his fire and his claws – fearsome great claws," Donald shuddered.

"A Knight has chain mail from head to foot," explained

Matilda, "even round his neck, and chain mail gauntlets; and you haven't armour for your horse."

"For my *horse*?"

"Certainly, if he has to meet a dragon." Angus Og was silent; his war horse had a breast plate but, "He has to have his head and neck protected and his flanks," said Matilda.

"Well, I'll be danged," said Angus Og.

They had to send to Carlisle, which is over the border in England, to get the Knight. His name was Robert le Douce; 'douce' in French means sweet and gentle, and Lady Matilda knew he would kill the Dragon as kindly as he could. Angus Og thought she had said "Robert le Deuce," which means Robert the Devil, so he was satisfied too.

"But what price does he want?" asked Donald. "He must have asked a price."

The price had left Angus Og so astounded he had nearly said, "I'll keep the Dragon. "A bag of gold," he told Donald, "to weigh as much as a month old lamb."

"Maybe we can find a wee bit lamb."

"Ours are all fat and fine," said Angus gloomily.

"We could put pebbles in the bag."

"He'll empty it out and count it."

"Well ... let him kill the Dragon first," said Donald.

Robert le Douce came riding to the river. He was clad in armour as Matilda had said, chain mail beautifully fitted and strongly made that glinted in the sun. In his helmet he had a red plume and his big prancing horse, white as milk, had red trappings too over the silver of its armour. They were attended by Sir Robert's squire, in chain armour too, but wearing a long white tunic edged with red; he carried a pennant with a red lion on white. Behind came two pages, in doublet and hose which are long stockings, one leg white and one red. The pages had short red velvet cloaks, feathered hats, and their hair was in curls. The men of Og in their short rough woven kirtles or kilts, their thick tunics and rawhide boots gasped when they saw them – not even Lady Matilda wore velvet.

It had been arranged that when Sir Robert reached the pool, a bullock, "Just one, mind," said Angus Og, would be driven into the meadow close to the river. "The Dragon has'nae eaten for two, three weeks or more. He's bound to come up," said Donald.

"Oh! oh!" cried Matilda. "No! Please, no," but it was no use crying "No." Angus Og had made up his mind and so, "If he has to be killed. . ." as Matilda said it she choked. "If. . .there's just one place that a sword can pierce a dragon," she forced herself to say it for the Dragon's sake so that he would not suffer too long. "One place, and that is under his throat, just above his heart," – as she said it she could not help tears falling and her tears too were like pearls but small ones. "I pray Sir Robert will find it quickly."

All the women and children were shut up in the Castle, Matilda in her tower room. She was so slim she could easily have climbed out of the window though it was barred, but thought it wiser to stay where she was. "Once menfolk are bent on fighting and killing, they have to go through with it," Edith had told her, which is true, but, "My Dragon. My dear, dear Dragon!" and Matilda put her hands over her ears and shut her eyes.

Robert le Douce killed the Dragon almost without a struggle; this was chiefly because the Dragon did not know he was supposed to struggle, far less to fight.

He had seen the bullock at once; he had come hopefully out of the river every day because by now he was excessively hungry and, "At last! My dinner!" He was crossing the river to get it when he was surprised by these terrible looking strangers and a horse that seemed to be covered in light which clinked as the horse moved. The man was shining too and, before the Dragon could blink, they were riding at him, the man with a sword that had a flashingly sharp point.

It is shaming to say that the Dragon would have run away, but they were between him and his dinner and he was so excessively hungry. He did let out one flame – it drove the pages back – but there was not time for more. Robert le Douce sprang from his horse – the Squire caught it – and from underneath the Dragon, which is the only way, the sword drove deep into the soft spot above his heart.

The Dragon gasped and sank to the ground; blood seemed to swim in his eyes, his coils threshed a little – Sir Robert was careful to keep away from his tail, but he need not have worried, the Dragon had not learnt how to use his tail. His claws gripped, then were still; the golden crest drooped, and the Dragon was dead.

Sir Robert was careful and thorough. He knew that dragons, even if their bodies were cut in two, could still join up and live again and, when he had cut off the Dragon's head, which was always the finish of a dragon fight, he called the cottar men to carry it and put it in the river far downstream so that it could not float back. They laid the rest of the Dragon quietly in the pool. Then Sir Robert rode up to the Castle to claim his reward.

"Where is Sir Robert?" asked Matilda. "I thought he would be dining with us."

There was no answer from Donald or Angus Og.

"I thought you would want to give a banquet for him," said Matilda. "We managed to save some of the salmon," and she had smoked salmon too, and smoked trout. There was a boar's head; a whole lamb was turning on the spit; a goose and chickens were cooking as well as a jugged hare. A good smell of onions and herbs filled the Castle and all day the cooks had been making pastries with almonds and honey. There were prunes, oranges and lemons. The board was set with, at each place, a great manchet or slice of bread on which to put the meat and a silver goblet; each guest would bring his knife, and Matilda had trained a servant who, at the end of the banquet, would carry round an ewer of hot water – "Scented!" said the women – a clean napkin over his arm and, as a silver basin was passed from place to place, he poured the hot water so that the guests could wash their hands and dry them on the napkin. "Did ye ever hear the like?" said the women. "Not one allowed to lick his fingers and thumb!" There was even ale for the Knight's horses, "and she talks to him in *French*!" The women were beginning to think there was nothing their Lady could not do but, "Where is Sir Robert?" asked Matilda now. "Isn't he coming?"

There was silence from Angus Og and, "I had best away home," said Donald.

Lady Matilda looked at them and her green eyes grew stern. "What have you two been up to?" She looked from one to the other of them. Angus Og was still tongue tied and, "You haven't paid Sir Robert," said Matilda. "You haven't given him his bag of honest gold."

"Well, the Dragon's dead," muttered Donald. "It seemed a waste."

Angus Og still said nothing; he looked at the ground.

"Of all the dishonourable, disgraceful, despicable, deceitful doings," said Matilda.

"It – it seemed a waste," Donald said it again, but feebly, and, "Go," ordered Matilda. "Go from here. You shall never set foot in this Castle again as long as I am its Mistress."

Donald slunk out, "And I want no part with you either," Matilda said to Angus Og. She drew her skirts away from him: "I am going to my room," and that is where she went and barred the door and stayed there for a week.

Angus Og could not bear it. Every other hour he went to her door, Brag padding after him. "Matilda. Tilda ... Tilda please," he called. No answer. He could hear her spinning or the angry plock in and out as she worked at her embroidery frame. "Tilda." No answer, then one day he called through the door, "Matilda – I have sent Sir Robert his bag of gold."

The spinning stopped and her voice asked, "What did he do?"

"He – sent it back," Angus Og gulped. He had never been as shamed. "He sent it back."

"Naturally," came Matilda's voice. "A noble Knight would have no truck with a cheat."

At that, strong man as he was, Angus Og felt his eyes hot with tears. "Tilda," he whispered through the keyhole. "Please have truck with me."

There was a pause. Then she said, "Will you behave as a

45

lord should? Will you dismiss Donald?"

"How can I dismiss Donald when he only did what I did?"

"That was spoken like a man," said Matilda and she unbarred the door.

Perhaps Robert le Douce was not as noble as Matilda thought. He had not deigned to haggle with Angus Og and, without a word, had gone to his horse which his Squire again was holding; he mounted and rode away, his Squire and pages after him. Angus Og had stood in the door of the Castle and watched him go; he had not liked Sir Robert's silence and already he was not feeling comfortable.

Sir Robert rode straight to the Water of Milk, downstream to where the Dragon's head had been laid, and he and the Squire and pages dragged it ashore. There were no men to help them and the head was extremely heavy, so that they had to rope it to their four horses to drag – Sir Robert's pages always carried a coil of strong rope on their saddles; they had to wade into the river to fasten it and they left their cloaks on the bank, but their hose and their fine leather riding boots were soaked as was the Squire's tunic. They dragged the head along the bank back to the pool. The golden crest trailed in the mud but the Dragon's eyes were open as if he knew what they were doing, "And the head's still warm," said the Knight. "Pray God it will join."

When they came to the pool it was red with blood and, "Empty your drinking horns and fill them," said Sir Robert. "Dragon's blood is precious; it can cure blindness and other ills and it can dissolve gold."

He, the Squire and the pages filled their drinking horns and then Sir Robert watched as the others splashed into the pool,

but it was deep, the pages' doublets and the Squire's chain mail
were ruined, but they steered the head as close to the body as they
could and untied the ropes. "May you join up and live," said Sir
Robert to the Dragon, and he made the Knight's sign of the Cross
over the pool.

It was more than two months before Matilda could bring herself to walk beside the river and when, on a still September day, she came, she grew more and more sad as she neared the Dragon pool. The blood had long been washed away and the water was clear, so clear that when she stood and looked down she could see, reflected, every fold of her white overgown, red kirtle and the folds of her head dress, but she saw no sign of the Dragon, no scales or bones, no stench in the pool, and she wondered what had happened to his body. Could he have dissolved so quickly? Of course, he was magic, thought Matilda. Anything could have happened, but she had never imagined what was happening now.

A ripple had appeared on the pool; ripples are often made by a fish jumping, but this was too big for any fish; ripples can be blown by the wind into a circle of white, but this ripple was gold; another came, even larger, and it was turquoise, then there was an emerald ripple and another unmistakably royal blue and, "Dragon!" cried Matilda. "Dragon – are you there?"

A tip of a crest came in answer, crumpled but golden and, "Dragon – you *are* there!" cried Matilda.

"Just," said the Dragon.

"Come out of the water. Come out."

"How can I? I'm far too weak."

"Try," coaxed Matilda. "Try, dear Dragon!" And, at last, he came, dragging himself, and she saw indeed he was weak; his crest and his wings were drooping; he had grown so thin she could see his bones under his scales; his claws scrabbled on the pebbles and round his neck was a great red scar. The effort of coming out of the pool left him panting and his eyes closed as he lay at her feet. "Dragon! Dear Dragon! Poor Dragon!" crooned Matilda and he opened his eyes and gazed at her with all the love of a dragon's heart.

After a while he whispered, "But why? I don't understand. What happened?" Matilda could not bear to tell him why but she told him of Robert le Douce.

"Should . . . should I have done something about him?"

"Indeed you should. You should have fought him. Eaten him."

"How could I eat all that tin?"

"You should have belched your flames at him and sizzled him in his armour."

"But that would have hurt him terribly."

"Was there ever such a dragon?" asked Matilda but he had closed his eyes again and, "You must have something to eat, at once," said Matilda.

"I couldn't eat bullock. My throat's too sore."

"I'll make you a junket," said Matilda. "Lie there and sun yourself. I'll be as quick as I can."

When Matilda told Angus Og the Dragon was alive it was extraordinary: Angus Og neither roared or bellowed; he did not make a sound but walked slowly to his chair and sat down with a bump and it was several minutes before he whispered – Angus Og to whisper! – "It's no-canny av'a. No-canny!"

"Not at all,' said Matilda. "It's perfectly natural," and she warned, "Any more killing and I'm going back to my mother," but Angus Og hardly heard her.

"Alive!" he whispered. "Alive!"

"Yes, my Lord. God bless Sir Robert," Matilda had guessed what the Knight had done. "Well, I must away to my junkets," said Matilda.

Junket is what country people used to eat before they had ice-cream, some prefer it still. It is like a jelly made with milk, easy to swallow and Matilda made hers sweet with honey and flavoured it with nutmeg. She made two washtubs full. Donald and his sons had to carry them down to the river. "That's your penance," she told Donald.

"Delicious," said the Dragon as, cool and sweet, it slid down his throat. He ate both tubs full and, "I think I'll have some more," he said, but there was not any more until Matilda filled fresh tubs. "We shall have to buy more cows," she told Angus Og. "I am going to need gallons of milk."

After the next day's junket, the Dragon was stronger but still puzzled. "It was that Knight who put my head back?"

"Yes," said Matilda.

"So that I joined up like a worm?"

"Yes," said Matilda, and because he was feeling so sorry for himself, the Dragon shed more tears. "I thought I was a Dragon and I'm only a worm," he sobbed. "A miserable worm," but Matilda was not having any of that.

"Don't you dare despise a worm," she said. "Of course you are a dragon, but dragons come from worms, luckily for you. It was by the power of the worm in you that you could join up and live."

"I don't feel like living," whimpered the Dragon.

"Oh dear! Oh dear!" said Matilda. Then she had an inspiration. "Have you ever tasted mead?" she asked.

"Mead? What's mead?"

"It's a kind of wine made from honey," and she fetched him the Castle's biggest goblet full.

"M'mm!" said the Dragon, licking his lips. "*M'mmmm!*" but what is a goblet to a Dragon and Matilda had to get Donald to bring down a barrel.

After the Dragon had finished the barrel, he could not even stagger to his pool but lay on the bank and snored. Just like Angus Og when he has had two or three of his tankards, thought Matilda fondly. When Angus Og woke, he had often a sore head, but the Dragon felt much better, in fact he was frisky. "Can I have mead every day?" he asked. "But just now I feel like my dinner . . . a bullock?" he asked hopefully. There were plenty of bullocks because, when Angus Og thought the Dragon was dead, the cattle were let back into the meadows. For a while Matilda was silent and then she said, "When you come to think of it, Dragon, bullocks are made of grass and barley, so if I made you a barley broth and served it with grass, you would be eating bullock, wouldn't you?"

"Would I?" The Dragon was doubtful, but he would have done anything for Matilda, so he did not take a bullock and, when Donald and his sons carried down two cauldrons of broth he supped them dutifully and ate handfuls of grass. "But, you know," he said, "I think barley and grass taste much better *after* they have turned to bullock."

"He's right," said Donald. Donald's legs and arms were aching from carrying tubs and cauldrons and it was in a temper that he went up to see Angus Og. "Can ye n'ae learn a lesson?" scolded Donald. "Let him have his bullock."

"That I will not!" and Angus Og bellowed even louder. "No bullock! You heard me."

"Ay. We heard ye."

"We couldn't help it," said Matilda. "I wish – I wish we could."

"I'll make you a mish-mash," she told the Dragon. "That's my own special mix-up porridge, but I beat eggs into mine; I usually use a dozen but for you it will have to be a hundred. After it you shall have a pail of mead."

For three whole days, because he loved Matilda, the Dragon tried the mish-mash, but he left more and more at the bottom of the washtubs that Donald and his sons carried up and down, "Come wind, come rain," they grumbled. The cottar children finished up the mish-mash in a matter of seconds but, "Ye're running out of oatmeal," Edith warned Matilda, "And soon there'll be no more eggs," said the hen-wives.

To turn the Dragon away from bullock, Matilda tried everything she could think of. "Nuts are tasty," she told the Dragon. "Let's ask the squirrels for nuts."

"Have you ever known a squirrel part with a nut?" asked the Dragon. Matilda had to confess she had never had and, "Anyway, it would take bushels," she said. The Dragon still had junket but the cows were running dry and the bees had no more honey, but Angus Og still thundered, "No bullock!"

"What am I to do?" said Matilda.

"Neeps are nice," suggested Edith.

In Scotland, turnips are called neeps. At that time they were new-fangled, but Angus Og had a whole field of neeps. "I'll boil them and mash them with butter," said Matilda hopefully. "Butter and herbs, nutmeg and salt."

"It *sounds* nice," said the Dragon.

In the Castle, Matilda was not at all popular. "Them neeps was for the sheep," said the shepherd and, "Do you know how long it took us to churn all that butter?" the dairy-women asked and, "Neeps are heavier by far than mish-mash," said Donald and warned her. "We're tired out wi' carrying cauldrons, me and my sons."

The Dragon took one mouthful of neeps and spat it straight out. A dragon's spit is like a large fountain and when it landed it made quite a hillock of neeps. There was a race between the cottar children and the sheep to see who could get there first; the cottar children won. "No more neeps," gasped the Dragon – his flanks were still heaving. "*Please*, no neeps."

Matilda stroked his head – to tell the truth she did not much like neeps herself. "I'm sorry. I'm only trying to make your peace with Angus Og," and the Dragon said, "Could Angus Og not make peace with me?"

Angus Og sat brooding in his great chair; every now and then he tugged his great red beard and wearily shut his eyes. He wished he could shut his ears as well.

"We're out of oatmeal," Edith angrily rattled her keys, "and there's hardly any salt. Do ye know the price of salt?"

"The cows cannae give all this milk," scolded the dairy-women, "and we can't churn any more butter. Ye'll see. *She*'ll be at the bog-butter next."

Bog-butter is butter mixed with wild garlic and buried under peat for a year. It is a great delicacy and, "Oh no!" groaned Angus Og.

"Oh, yes!" shrilled the dairy-women and, "The hens have run out of eggs." The hen-wives were even shriller.

"The sheep'll not go through the winter with what neeps are left," said the shepherd.

"The bees have no more honey so we cannae make more mead," the taverner, who looked after the wine was worried. "There's but half a hogs-head left."

"Did you say *half*?" Angus Og sat up straight.

"And how long will that last?" asked the taverner. "*She* gives him a pailful a day." Angus Og winced.

Finally there was Donald. "Have *you* come to girn as well?" asked Angus Og.

"Ay," said Donald. "Ay. I'm doing no more hauling, I warn ye, no carting of cauldrons and wash tubs, I and my sons neither. If the Dragon wants his dinner he can come and get it," said Donald.

"But that means he'll invade us."

"Ay, but not us," said Donald. "We're leaving, I and my sons – all of us."

As most of Angus Og's men-at-arms and free-men were Donald's uncles, or brothers or sons, or cousins from first cousins to twelfth, Og would be left without men, and "the women gae

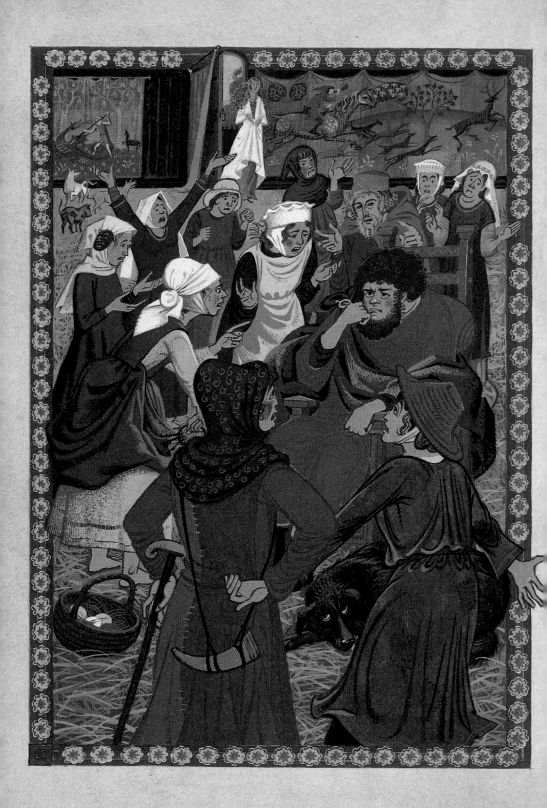

with us," warned Donald.

No men and no women so, of course, no children to pat on the head or take up on the saddle; no trout or salmon: no eggs and no milk and no butter: no oatmeal: presently no salt or turnips: no honey, soon no mead, and, "What is a man to do?" groaned Angus Og.

"Give over," said Donald.

"Give *over*?"

"Ay."

"Ogs never give over."

"But they could do something new," suggested Matilda.

"And what is that?" demanded Angus Og.

"Something an Og seems never able to have done," said Matilda.

"And what is that? That an Og cannot do? Tell me that. Speak woman. What cannot I do?"

"Make peace," said Matilda.

Angus Og sank back in his chair and tugged again at his beard. The angry voices still sounded in his ears and he still did not feel comfortable about Sir Robert. He pulled his beard, then ruffled his hair and bit his lip. Then, "The devil haet!" swore Angus Og. "Let the Dragon have his bullock."

The bullocks did not mind. "What difference is there?" they would have said – if they had ever said anything – "between being driven in for Angus Og's dinner – or the Sunday joint – and being snapped up by the Dragon?" As a matter of fact, walking into the glow of his eyes, seized by his claws and carried up by his wings was rather like going to heaven. "And he only takes one every three weeks," said Matilda.

"One is enough," said the Dragon.

This was all a long time ago. Angus Og and Matilda lie in the churchyard now, and all the little Angus Ogs and Matildas. On the hill there is no Castle, only an ordinary house and where the bailey used to be there is a garden. The meadows are still rich in grass and clover though the forests are only woods, but the Water of Milk still runs and the big pool is there; people say so is the Dragon but no one has seen him which is not surprising as he is now very old and spends most of his time asleep.

Now and again, the taste comes back to him of junket and mead; then he gives a sigh that sets the pool water swirling. People think it is the wind, but it is the Dragon. Now and again a bullock is missing, but it might have strayed; a sheep too, but it might have been taken by foxes – yet it is strange that, in that pool and in all that stretch of the river, no one, though they come fishing, has ever caught a salmon or a trout; and still somebody walks along the river hoping to see an emerald ripple or the tip of a golden crest.

This story comes from an old, old legend of Tundergarth and Corrie; it is not the same as the legend but this is how it came to me and may well have been true – many people round about still believe in dragons.

I should like to thank Mr. A. E. Truckell, M.B.E., M.A., F.S.A., F.S.A.(Scot.), F.M.A., Curator of Museums, for the help and advice he gave me from his vast treasury of knowledge, not only in history but in dragon-lore.

R.G.